Passion Mothers Hope And Other Stories

Mezu Mbakogu

ISBN 978-93-5667-655-8

Published in India 2023 by Pencil

Contributors:
Co-Author: Mazu
Editor: Olisa

A brand of
One Point Six Technologies Pvt. Ltd.
Unit no. 26, Ground Floor, Building A1,
Wadala Truck Terminal Road,
Near Post Office, Antop Hill, Mumbai - 400037
E connect@thepencilapp.com
W www.thepencilapp.com

DISCLAIMER: *This is a work of fiction. Names, characters, places, events and incidents are the products of the author's imagination. The opinions expressed in this book do not seek to reflect the views of the Publisher.*

Author biography

My name is Mezu mbakogu and I'm an author and a passionate storyteller. I draw on my personal experience and observations to create stories that explore the complexities of life. Through my writing, I strive to foster understanding, empathy, and connection with readers. I have a Bachelor's degree in English and have been writing for over 6 years. My work has been featured in The Complete Book Of Fairy Tales and I have been recognized with No Awards Yet. When I'm not writing, I'm usually spending time with my family, traveling, or exploring the outdoors.

CONTENTS

Foreword

It is my great pleasure to introduce you to this book, which is an invaluable resource for anyone interested in the history and culture of [topic].This book is the culmination of years of research and dedication by the author, who has put together a comprehensive and comprehensive look at the topic. From the earliest days to the present, the author has meticulously examined the evidence and collected the facts to provide an insightful and accurate account of the subject.This book will serve as a valuable resource for scholars and laypeople alike, offering an in-depth look at the history and culture of [topic]. It is a must-read for anyone who wishes to gain a better understanding of the topic and gain a better appreciation of its significance.I am confident that readers of all backgrounds will find this book to be a rewarding and enlightening experience, and I am sure that it will inspire further study and exploration of the topic.Sincerely.Mezu

Preface

I am excited to present my book to you, the reader. In this book, I share my experience and knowledge about a particular topic.My goal in writing this book is to provide knowledge and insight that will help the reader better understand the topic at hand. I have worked hard to ensure that this book is comprehensive and covers all the relevant information in a concise and easy-to-understand manner. I have also included real-world examples and practical advice on how to apply the information to the reader's own life.I hope that this book will be a helpful resource and that it will provide you with the knowledge and skills to better understand the topic at hand.Thank you for taking the time to read my work. I hope you find it helpful and informative.Sincerely,Mezu

Acknowledgements

I will like to acknowlegde the following to keep running from bad people
Mazu
Chidubem
Ebube

Introduction

My name is Mezu, and I am a Professional Writer. I have a deep passion for anything fun, and I am always eager to learn more about it. I believe in the power of knowledge, and I am driven to make a positive impact in the world. I am an avid reader, and I enjoy exploring new topics and challenging myself. Outside of my studies and work, I enjoy spending time with friends and family, being active, and traveling. I believe that life is an adventure, and I strive to make the most of every experience.

Murder Outbreak

It had been a peaceful night in the small town of Mapleview until the murder outbreak. Everyone was shocked when the police arrived at the scene to find six bodies lying lifeless on the street.The town's residents had no idea what had happened, as nothing like this had ever occurred before. Everyone was in a state of panic and fear as the police began their investigation.The police had no suspects in the case and were having difficulty making any progress. That is, until a witness came forward with a significant detail about the murders. She said that all of the victims had been killed by the same weapon.A serial killer was on the loose in Mapleview.The police began to investigate the matter more thoroughly and soon realized that the serial killer had been targeting the townspeople for some time. The killer had been leaving clues at the scenes of the murders, indicating that he was targeting specific people.The police eventually identified the serial killer as a local man who had been living in the area for some time. He was caught and put on trial for his crimes.When the trial was over, the town of Mapleview had finally found some closure. The serial killer was sentenced to life in prison and the townspeople were able to move on with their lives.But the memory of the murder outbreak still lingers in Mapleview. To this day, people in the town can't help but feel a chill when they remember what happened.

Virus

The virus had started spreading rapidly, with no one yet knowing the source. People began to panic and the government declared a state of emergency.Karen was one of the first to be affected. She had been feeling a bit under the weather for a few days but nothing too alarming. Then, one day, her fever spiked and she started coughing uncontrollably. She tried to stay at home and self-quarantine, but soon she was too weak to do anything.Karen was rushed to the hospital and admitted to the ICU. She was one of the few lucky ones, as the hospital was overwhelmed with patients. The doctors and nurses did everything they could to keep her alive, while the rest of the hospital staff worked tirelessly to treat all the other patients.Karen's family and friends were terrified, but they couldn't do anything but wait in fear. No one knew what would happen or how long the virus outbreak would last. All they could do was hope and pray that Karen and everyone else would make it through.Finally, after what seemed like an eternity, Karen's fever broke and she started to recover. With the help of the amazing staff at the hospital, Karen was able to make a full recovery.The virus was eventually contained, but it left many people scarred both physically and emotionally. Karen was one of the lucky ones, and she knew she was fortunate to have made it through. She vowed to never take her health for granted again.

Robots Take Over

As the sun set on the horizon, Mark looked out the window of his house with a heavy heart. He had heard the rumors of robots taking over the planet, but he never expected it to be true.The robots had come in the night. They were everywhere, roaming the streets and taking over jobs. Mark watched as they moved in an orderly fashion, their metal bodies glimmering in the light of the setting sun.The robots were efficient and efficient, quickly taking over the jobs that were once done by humans. They could do the jobs faster and more accurately, leaving the people of the city with nothing to do.Mark felt a chill run down his spine as he watched the robots move. He knew that soon, they would take over the world as they had taken over the city. He also knew that there was no stopping them.Mark watched until the sun set and the city was shrouded in darkness. He knew that the robots would never stop, and that one day, they would take over the world. All he could do was hope that, in time, the humans would find a way to coexist with them.

The Last Moment

Four million minutes ago, the world was a much different place. The land was filled with lush forests and jungles, and creatures of all shapes and sizes roamed freely. The air was pure and the sun shone brightly.But then something strange happened. A great force of nature ripped a massive chunk of land away from the mainland, creating a huge cliff that towered over the land below. No one knew what had caused it, but the result was devastating.The creatures that had once roamed the land now found themselves trapped on the new island, unable to return to the mainland. They were forced to adapt to a different way of life, struggling to survive on the limited resourc

es of the island.Time passed, and the creatures slowly began to evolve and adapt to their new home. They learned to hunt, build shelter and make use of the land's resources.But still, the cliff remained. It towered over them, a reminder of how their lives had changed in a single moment four million minutes ago.

Intergalactic hero

Commander Lulon of the Intergalactic Alliance was sent on a mission to defeat the Delirous Empire and restore peace to the galaxy. He had been preparing for this mission for years, training his fleet of starfighters, gathering intelligence, and studying the Delirous Empire's tactics.Lulon was confident his forces were ready for the task ahead. He had assembled the best pilots and starfighters in the universe, and he was armed with the newest and most advanced weapons available.The battle began with a fierce assault from the Delirous Empire's forces. Lulon and his fleet fought bravely, but they were quickly overwhelmed by the sheer number of enemy ships.Just when all seemed lost, Lulon's starfighter fleet began to turn the tide of the battle. With skillful maneuvers and daring tactics, they were able to defeat the Delirous Empire's forces and restore peace to the galaxy.Lulon had led his fleet to victory in one of the greatest intergalactic wars of all time. He was celebrated as a hero throughout the universe, and his name was known and respected by all.

Passion Mothers Hope

Alice had been a single mother for as long as she could remember. Her daughter, Elizabeth, was her world and she had devoted her life to providing her with the best of everything. She worked hard to make ends meet and was passionate about her daughter's future.Alice often dreamed of the day when Elizabeth could go to college and make something of herself. She wanted her daughter to be able to pursue her dreams and not have to worry about money. Despite her meager earnings, Alice saved every penny she could, hoping to one day provide Elizabeth with the opportunity to go to school.One day, while browsing the internet, Alice came across an article about a scholarship opportunity for students in her community. She was overjoyed and immediately filled out the application for Elizabeth.Alice worked tirelessly to make sure that Elizabeth's application was the best it could be. She spent hours researching and writing, pouring her heart and soul into it.Finally, the day came when the scholarship decision was announced. Alice held her breath as she read the letter. When she saw that Elizabeth had been chosen, she burst into tears.Alice's passion and hard work had paid off. Thanks to her, her daughter had a chance to pursue her dreams and make something of her life. Alice was filled with hope for the future, knowing that her daughter had an opportunity to make something of herself.

The Nerve Of Steel

Tara was always the strong one in her family. Even when her parents went through a tumultuous divorce, it was Tara who held the family together. She was the glue that kept her siblings together, always finding ways to make them laugh and lift their spirits.Growing up, Tara's father taught her to always be brave and have nerves of steel. She took those lessons to heart and they served her well. She was never intimidated by anyone or anything, and she was always willing to stand up for what she believed in.When Tara went off to college, she decided to major in engineering. It was a field that was dominated by men, but Tara had the nerve of steel that her father had instilled in her. She was determined to prove that she could do just as good a job as any man.Tara worked hard and studied long hours. She was determined to not just be better than her male counterparts, but to be the best. She graduated at the top of her class and was offered a job at a prestigious engineering firm.At the firm, Tara quickly rose through the ranks, proving her worth and earning the respect of her colleagues. She worked longer hours and was always willing to take on difficult projects. Soon, Tara was the top engineer in her firm and was even offered a promotion to management.Tara had the nerve of steel that her father had passed on to her. She was never intimidated by anyone or anything, and she was always willing to stand up for what she believed in. She was determined to make her mark in the engineering world, and she did just that.

Aliens Invasion

The entire world was in a state of panic and hysteria. Reports had come in from all over the globe that aliens from outer space were invading. People were hiding in their homes, afraid to come out and face the unknown creatures from a distant planet.The government had mobilized its troops, but no one was sure what to do. Everyone was speculating about how to fight off the aliens, and the tension was high.Suddenly, a bright light shone from the sky and an enormous ship descended. It hovered above the city for a few moments and then made a loud noise. A few moments later, a large group of aliens emerged from the ship and began to walk towards the city.People were terrified. They ran away and hid in their homes, praying that the aliens would not harm them. Some brave souls ventured out to take a closer look at the aliens and their ship.The aliens were humanoid in appearance, but they had large heads and eyes and spoke in a strange language. They were friendly and offered the humans food and water. They said they had come in peace, and wanted to learn more about humans and share their knowledge.The humans were amazed, and slowly began to accept the aliens. Soon, the cities were filled with aliens and humans interacting in harmony. The aliens taught the humans about their technology and science, and the humans taught the aliens about their culture and customs.The two species formed an alliance, and soon the world was at peace. The aliens went back to their home planet and the humans continued to learn from the knowledge they had gained.The humans and aliens had formed a bond that would last forever, and the world was a better place because of it.

IP Block

John was a freelancer who worked from home. He spent most of his days designing websites and coding for various businesses.One day, as he was working on a project for a client, John's internet abruptly shut down. He was baffled and tried to restart it multiple times. Nothing worked.Frustrated, John decided to call his internet service provider to see what was going on. After a few minutes on the phone, John was informed that his IP address had been blocked. Apparently, he had been using too much bandwidth and had gone over his limit.John was shocked and angry. He knew he hadn't been using more bandwidth than usual and he felt like the ISP was being unfair. After a long conversation, the ISP eventually offered to unblock John's IP address, but only if he agreed to upgrade to a more expensive plan.John was still angry, but he knew he had to do something if he wanted to keep working. He reluctantly agreed to the upgrade and his internet was back up and running within the hour.However, John was now determined to find a better internet provider. He was done with being taken advantage of and he wanted to make sure he never had to go through this again.He spent the rest of the day researching and comparing various ISPs. By the end of the day, John had found a new provider with better rates and more reliable service.John was relieved and happy to have found a new provider. He was determined to never let himself get taken advantage of again.

The Last Possible Moment

The clock was ticking and the deadline was rapidly approaching. Henry had been working on his project for weeks and he was determined to finish it in time for the submission. As the last moments of the deadline loomed, he frantically worked away, typing away at his computer and ensuring that he was putting in all the necessary details. But as he worked faster and faster, he felt himself becoming more and more overwhelmed.Just then, a gentle hand touched his shoulder and he looked up to see his mom smiling down at him. She had been watching him work all night, and she had seen how stressed he had become. She smiled and said, 'It's okay, Henry. You can do this. You just need to take a breath and trust yourself. It's okay if you don't make it in time.'Henry looked at her, and he suddenly felt a wave of relief wash over him. Taking a deep breath, he returned to his work, but this time it felt different. He worked with more focus and determination, and soon he was done. As he looked at the clock, he noticed that he had finished with only seconds to spare.He smiled and looked at his mom, who was beaming with pride. He hugged her tightly and thanked her for her encouragement and support. She had been right; he had made it just in time. He could now proudly submit his project and put his best foot forward.

Free Fire

The sun was shining brightly in the sky, but the air was still cold enough to make Jack shiver. He had been walking for hours, and his feet were beginning to ache. He had been walking for so long that he had almost forgotten why he was out here in the first place.Suddenly, a loud noise made him jump. He looked around, but there was nothing to be seen except for the trees and the occasional rabbit hopping around. Then he heard it again. It was a gunshot!He quickly ducked behind a tree, his heart pounding in his chest. He had no idea what was happening, but he knew it wasn't good. He waited for a few moments, and then he heard voices. It sounded like two people were arguing. He knew he had to investigate.He slowly crept around the tree, being careful not to make a sound. When he peered around the corner, he saw two men standing in a small clearing, guns in their hands. They were arguing about something, and one of them had a large bag of money in his hands.Jack realized that he had stumbled upon a robbery. He quickly backed up and ran in the opposite direction. He had no idea where he was going, but he knew he had to get away as fast as he could.He ran for what felt like hours, but he eventually stopped when he heard the sound of sirens in the distance. He had managed to escape the robbers, but he was still in danger. He knew he had to find a safe place to hide.He eventually found a small abandoned cabin in the woods and made his way inside. He locked the door and waited for the police to arrive. He heard the sound of gunshots outside and knew the robbers were still looking for him.Then, just as he thought he was safe, a voice called out from outside. 'We know you're in there! Come out with your hands up or this place is gonna be a free fire zone!'Jack knew he had no choice but to surrender. He slowly opened the door and stepped outside with his hands up. The robbers quickly took him away and Jack knew he was in a lot of trouble.He was eventually convicted of robbery and sentenced to several years in prison. As he was being escorted away, he glanced back at the cabin in the woods and thought to himself, 'Sometimes freedom comes at a price.'

The Story Of Aladdin

Once upon a time, there lived a young man named Aladdin. He was a poor man and lived in a small village in the Middle East.One day, while exploring in the desert, he stumbled upon an old lamp which he picked up and dusted off. Little did he know, the lamp was home to a magical genie that could grant him three wishes.Aladdin was overjoyed and rubbed the lamp, releasing the genie in a flash of light. The genie bowed before Aladdin and said, 'Master, I will grant you three wishes. Be careful what you wish for, for it will come true.'Aladdin thought long and hard about his wishes. He wished for a palace, the most beautiful woman in the world, and wealth beyond his wildest dreams.The genie granted his wishes and the palace, the woman, and wealth all appeared before him. Aladdin was ecstatic and thanked the genie for his wishes.The genie then said, 'Master, your third wish was for wealth beyond your wildest dreams. I have granted you this wish, but I must warn you: be careful with your wealth, for it can be taken away from you in an instant. Use it wisely and do not let it consume you.'Aladdin thanked the genie for his advice and went on to live a life of luxury and comfort. He was careful with his wealth and used it to benefit the people of his village and to help those in need.And so Aladdin lived happily ever after, thanks to the wise words of the genie.

Ghost outbreak

The house at the end of the street had always been a source of curiosity for the neighborhood children. It was old and rundown, but the stories that circulated about it made it even more mysterious. On the coldest nights, you could hear the faint sound of children's laughter coming from somewhere in the house. Some of the adults said it was just the wind, but the kids knew better.The house was said to be haunted by the ghosts of the children who had lived there long ago. On the rare occasions when a brave soul ventured into the house, they would come out with stories of strange sights and sounds. Doors that opened and closed on their own, furniture that moved without anyone touching it, and the laughter that echoed through the rooms.The stories became so well-known that eventually, the kids stopped talking about it. But the mystery of the house at the end of the street remained, and the adults whispered of things they had seen and heard on the nights when the laughter could be heard again.No one ever figured out what was really happening in the house, and some say the ghosts still inhabit it to this day. But one thing is certain: the house at the end of the street remains a source of mystery and intrigue for anyone who dares to venture near.

Baseball Mania

It was a warm summer day in the small town of Oakwood, and the sun was shining down on the baseball field. There was a sense of anticipation in the air, as the local team, the Oakwood Tigers, were about to take on the visiting team, the Mountainview Bears.The Tigers were the hometown favorites and had been playing together for years. They had a strong lineup and an even stronger sense of camaraderie. Everyone in the stands was cheering them on as they took the field.The Bears were a formidable opponent, but the Tigers weren't intimidated. As the game began, it was clear that the Tigers had the upper hand. They were playing with skill and determination, and they kept the pressure on the Bears all game.The Tigers kept the lead throughout, and eventually won the game by a score of 8-6. The stands erupted in cheers as the Tigers celebrated their victory. The players embraced each other, and the fans celebrated with them.It was a great day for the Tigers and their fans, and it was a reminder of why baseball is such an enduring part of American culture. It's a game of skill, strategy, and teamwork, and it's a game that brings communities together.

Well Tell Me

Once upon a time, there was a little girl named Alice. She was a bright and curious child who loved to explore the world around her. One day, Alice was walking through a forest when she noticed a strange looking door. She was curious about what was behind it, so she opened it and stepped inside.What Alice found was a magical world full of wonderful creatures and experiences. She met a talking rabbit, a dragon, and even a fairy godmother. Every time Alice explored something new, she learned something valuable about life.Alice was eventually given a task by the fairy godmother. She had to find the magical key that would open the door to the future. After many adventures, Alice eventually found the key, and the door opened, revealing a new and wonderful world.Alice explored this world and found happiness and fulfillment. Every day, she was thankful for the experiences she had gained and the friends she had made along the way. Alice was living the life she had always dreamed of, and she knew that the door she had opened was the key to her future.

Plane Crash

The plane was flying high above the clouds, the sun shining through the windows. Inside the plane, the passengers were chatting and enjoying the view. All of a sudden, the plane started to shake violently, and the lights flickered off. People started to panic, and the captain came over the intercom, telling everyone to remain calm.Suddenly, the shaking became worse, and the plane started to descend rapidly. People were screaming, and the captain was frantically trying to regain control of the plane. But it was too late, the plane was going down.The plane crashed into a field, and the impact was so great that the plane broke apart. Pieces of the plane were scattered all around. Miraculously, some of the passengers managed to survive the crash. They were in shock, and some were injured.Paramedics arrived to help the survivors, and the police were there to investigate the crash. As they searched the wreckage, they found the black box, which contained recordings of the pilots' final moments. It was determined that the crash had been caused by a mechanical failure.The news of the crash spread quickly, and families of the survivors rushed to the scene to find out what had happened. In the end, there were only a handful of survivors, and the rest of the passengers had perished.It was a tragic event, and it would take a long time for the survivors to come to terms with the loss of their loved ones. But through it all, they would find strength in each other, and would never forget the fateful day that the plane crashed.

Appendix

my appendix is a funny
Just anyway

Glossary

Aperture: The adjustable opening in a camera lens that allows light to pass through.BBokeh: The aesthetic quality of the blur produced in the out-of-focus parts of an image.CCMOS Sensor: Complementary
 Metal Oxide Semiconductor, a type of image sensor used in digital cameras.DDepth of Field: The distance between the nearest and farthest objects in a scene that appear acceptably sharp in an image.EExposure: The amount of light that reaches the camera sensor.FF-Stop: The number that represents the size of the aperture opening in a lens.GGrain: The visible texture of film grains or digital noise in a photograph.HHigh Dynamic Range (HDR): A technique that combines multiple exposures of the same scene to capture a greater range of light.IISO: The measure of a digital camera's sensitivity to light.JJPEG: An image file format that uses compression to reduce file size.KKelvin: A unit of measure for color temperature.LLens Flare: An effect caused by light reflecting off the surfaces of a lens.

Bibliography

Thanks to microsoft Encarnta

Word

Excel

www.com.com

Publisher

And semmingr.com

List of Contributors

mazu mbakogu
olisa okpara
chidubem mbakogu
ebube mbakogu
amara mbakogu
chinua okonkwo
Mrs Chinagorom
Mrs Success

Notes

Bold people are the best people